The Patience Song

by Dr. Crystal Bowe

Illustrations by Mike Motz

To my inspirations,
my loves, my children!

The Patience Song

by
Dr. Crystal Bowe

Illustrations by Mike Motz

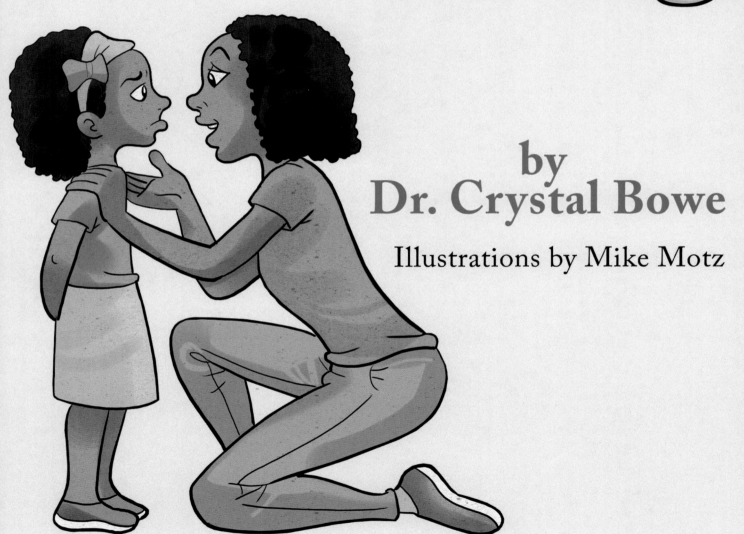

Little Isabel was a sweet and happy girl.
She loved to laugh and loved to play.
She was kind to everyone she met.
However, little Isabel hated to wait!

One day, when little Isabel finished her homework,
She noticed her tummy rumbling.
She was hungry!
So she went to the kitchen to get a snack.

Her daddy was in the kitchen, cooking dinner.
He told Isabel to wait until dinner was ready.
Isabel got upset.
She was hungry now!

So Isabel's mom sat her down and sang her a song:

Patient, patient, you have to be real patient,
When Daddy is cooking up your food,
you have to be real patient.

One day, Isabel was outside playing
with her brother.
He was shooting the basketball with his friends,
and Isabel wanted to play.
Her brother said, "I will play with
you when my friends leave."
Isabel got upset.
She wanted to play now!

So Isabel's mom came outside with Isabel
and sang her a song:

Patient, patient, you have to be real patient,
When your brother is playing with his friends,
you have to be real patient.

Later that summer, Isabel went
to the amusement park with her dad.
She was finally tall enough to ride a roller coaster!
But when she and Daddy got to the ride,
the line was so long!
Isabel got upset.
She wanted to ride now!

But quietly in her ear, her dad sang her a song:

Patient, patient, you have to be real patient,
When you're waiting for your turn to ride,
you have to be real patient.

On a sunny afternoon, Isabel was in the car with her dad.
He had picked her up from school and was rushing to get her to her piano lesson.
He said, "I do not want you to be late!"
Her dad was upset.
He wanted her to be there now!

Isabel smiled. From the backseat,
she sang her dad a song:

Patient, patient, you have to be real patient,
When you want to get me there on time,
you have to be real patient.

Her dad smiled.

One holiday season, Isabel was out shopping.
She had saved her money to get a gift for her mom!
She found a painting that was perfect!
She wrapped the present and put it under the tree.
When her mom saw the present, she was so excited!
Isabel's mom wanted to open her present now!

Isabel laughed, and gave her mom a hug.
In her mom's ear, she sang:

Patient, patient, you have to be real patient,
When you want to get your gift,
you have to be real patient.

Isabel's mom hugged her and laughed.
"Now YOU are the patience expert!"

The Patience Song

Pa tient,   pa   tient, You have to be   pa   tient. Re gard less of

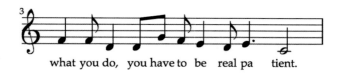

what you do, you have to be real pa   tient.

Made in the USA
Coppell, TX
29 August 2020

35560569R00019